Angelina Ballerina™

Tip-Top Christmas Crafts

Based on the text by **Katharine Holabird** Illustrations by **Helen Craig**

Grosset & Dunlap

GROSSET & DUNLAP
Published by the Penguin Group
Penguin Group (USA) Inc., 375 Hudson Street, New York, New York 10014, U.S.A.
Penguin Group (Canada), 90 Eglinton Avenue East, Suite 700, Toronto, Ontario, Canada M4P 2Y3
(a division of Pearson Penguin Canada Inc.)
Penguin Books Ltd, 80 Strand, London WC2R 0RL, England
Penguin Ireland, 25 St Stephen's Green, Dublin 2, Ireland
(a division of Penguin Books Ltd)
Penguin Group (Australia), 250 Camberwell Road, Camberwell, Victoria 3124, Australia
(a division of Pearson Australia Group Pty Ltd)
Penguin Books India Pvt Ltd, 11 Community Centre, Panchsheel Park, New Delhi - 110 017, India
Penguin Group (NZ), Cnr Airborne and Rosedale Roads, Albany, Auckland 1310, New Zealand
(a division of Pearson New Zealand Ltd)
Penguin Books (South Africa) (Pty) Ltd, 24 Sturdee Avenue, Rosebank, Johannesburg 2196, South Africa

Penguin Books Ltd, Registered Offices:
80 Strand, London WC2R 0RL, England

ISBN 0-448-44387-2   10 9 8 7 6 5 4 3 2 1

Get Ready...Get Set...Go!

Here are some ideas for holiday baking and crafts for you to do with a parent. Each page shows an example of the finished product, but don't worry if yours looks different—the memory of doing something together is what makes each activity special.

—Angelina

Angelina says:

1. Have a grown-up read through the instructions first and see what, if anything, can be done in advance and what materials are needed.

2. This helping hand symbol means that adult assistance is required. Of course, adult supervision is always recommended.

3. Do not use sharp knives or scissors unless a grown-up is helping you.

4. Never use an oven (even a microwave) or touch something hot by yourself.

5. Neatness counts! Wear a smock or apron, and tie back your hair. Remember to wash your hands before you cook and after you get messy from your hard work.

6. You're almost ready to begin! Now, be sure you have a clean, clear work surface, then gather all the materials you need before you get started!

7. Remember to clean everything up when you're done and to leave your work area the way you found it.

Table of Contents

Start with Angelina's Christmas Countdown, then do the rest of the crafts. By the time you're done with these crafts, you'll be all ready for Christmas!

Craft Projects

You can make a lot of projects with just a few basic items!
See the supply box on each page to find out what else you might need.
All supplies are available at your local craft store.

Beads and buttons—a variety of buttons and beads in all shapes and sizes will be fun to use to decorate your creations. You'll also want a small supply of pipe cleaners, pom-poms, rhinestones, sequins, and wiggle eyes.

Glue—try to use tacky *craft glue* when gluing tiny parts or pieces. The stickiness helps little fingers position pieces and keep them in place. To thin craft glue, mix it with water and paint it on with a paintbrush. Special *fabric glue* is great for gluing fabric. *Glue sticks* provide neat and easy gluing for paper projects.

Fabric, felt, and faux fur—use your imagination. Try different types of fabric.

Glitter—pick an assortment of colors for lots of different looks. To conserve your glitter, hold your project over a paper plate when you sprinkle it. Then fold the plate and pour the excess glitter back into the container.

Paint—you'll want to use *acrylic paint* for many projects. *Fabric paint* or 3-D *puff paint* comes in squeeze bottles for simple styling.

Ribbon, yarn, and thread—use whatever you have on hand.

Scissors—use small round-tipped scissors. Have an adult cut cork or fabric.

Tape—use masking tape, double-sided tape, or clear tape—whatever you have.

Templates—templates for several of Angelina's crafts are included at the back of the book. For other crafts, use cookie cutters to get the shapes you need.

# Cooking Projects

Candy decorations, chocolate chips, and edible glitter—lots of sweet stuff can be found at grocery or baking supply stores. Or use whatever you have too much of at home!

Cookie cutters—use your favorite holiday cutters (about 2-inch shapes work best), or have a grown-up cut around some of the punch-out templates found in the back of this book.

Measuring cups and spoons—it's fun to measure and pour! Practice counting as you go.

Wire rack—use to cool cookies or dry ornaments. A paper towel or flat paper bag will work, too.

Rolling pin, cookie sheets, and spatula— these are important for making cookies and some nonedible projects, too.

Ingredients—you can substitute margarine for butter and baking chocolate for chocolate chips, and of course, make your own peanut butter cracker sandwiches or shred your own sharp Cheddar cheese (just like Mrs. Mouseling!).

Plastic wrap, paper plates, wax paper, and zip-lock bags—you can often substitute one for another, too. Wax paper makes a perfect surface for most of Angelina's projects. When you're done, just toss the mess!

Oven mitts—you should have an adult handle everything that comes out of the oven or microwave. If you do work with anything hot, do NOT touch it without first putting on oven mitts.

Angelina's Christmas Countdown

Supplies:
- Pretty paper (at least 2 colors)
- Dark crayon or number stickers (1–25)
- Glue stick or tape
- Pretty ribbon

Angelina can't wait for Christmas—it seems so far away. But this pretty-colored paper chain helps her count the days.

How many days until Christmas?

1. Cut out 25 strips of colored paper. With crayon or stickers, number the strips from 1 to 25. Shape the number 1 strip into a circle and glue the ends.

2. Link the number 2 color strip through the first, and glue it into a circle so you're making a chain. Continue with the remaining 23 strips.

3 Cut out a special shape, and tape or glue the links to it (with the number 1 at the top).

4 Punch a hole in the top of your special shape and thread a ribbon through.

5 Hang the paper chain by a ribbon in a special spot. Then beginning on December 1, take one link off from the bottom each day . . . until it's Christmas Day!

Glitter Ornament

Supplies:
- Small Styrofoam ball
- Craft glue
- Glitter
- Beads
- Pipe cleaner

Angelina decorates her tree with balls of glitter and sparkling beads!

1 Paint the Styrofoam ball with thinned glue and sprinkle with glitter over a paper plate. Let dry. Re-glue and glitter any bare spots. Let dry again.

2 Poke beads into the ball to decorate them and add a pipe cleaner for a hanger.

3 Place your glittery ornaments on your tree and watch them sparkle!

Picture Perfect Ornament

Picture one of these precious ornaments on your tree!

1. Paint a mini craft box and let it dry. If desired, cover with thinned craft glue and sprinkle the box with glitter. Ask an adult to trim a photo to fit inside the box bottom.

2. Glue a small pom-pom inside the box, then glue the picture to the pom-pom to make it stand out. Use a pipe cleaner to make a hanger. Decorate your box with sequins and pom-poms to make it your own!

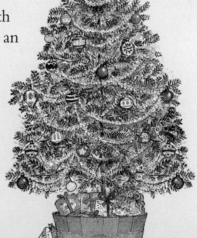

11

Soap Snowmouse

Supplies:
- Bar of white soap
- Peppercorns
- Twigs
- Ribbon

Angelina absolutely loves snowy days at Miller's Pond. After the holidays, bring this snowmouse into the tub for some good, clean fun!

1 Have a grown-up grate a bar of soap. Add a spoonful or two of water at a time, and stir until the mixture holds together but isn't too wet.

2 Make 3 soap balls for the body and head, and tiny soap balls for ears and a snout. Finish with peppercorn eyes and nose, twig arms, and a ribbon scarf.

13

Snowballs

Angelina made a huge snowball and hurled it at the boys. You won't want to throw these tasty snowballs, though!

Ingredients:

- 1 (12-ounce) package white chocolate chips
- 2 tablespoons vegetable shortening
- 1 box Ritz Bits peanut butter sandwiches
- White nonpareils

1 Have a grown-up melt chips and shortening in a microwave on medium-high for 1 minute. Stir. Microwave at additional 10-second intervals, stirring till smooth.

2 Dip cracker sandwiches into melted chocolate, first making sure the chocolate isn't too hot. Then roll in nonpareils and place on wax paper until set.

3 Enjoy these tasty, pretty snacks!

Easy Cheese Crackers

Angelina loves her mother's cheddar cheese pies more than anything in the world. These cheese crackers make a yummy bite-sized treat!

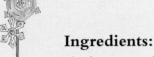

Ingredients:
- 2 sticks butter, softened
- 1 (8-ounce) bag shredded sharp Cheddar
- 2 cups flour
- 1 teaspoon salt
- 1½ cups crisp rice cereal

1 Mix butter and shredded cheese. Add flour and salt and mix well. Stir in cereal. Shape into small balls and place onto ungreased cookie sheet.

2 Press each cookie with a fork or your fingers until it is about ¼-inch thick. Have a grown-up bake at 400° for 12 to 15 minutes. Cool on rack.

Angelina's Cottage

Build a delicious miniature of Angelina's cozy cottage.

Supplies:
- ½ pound confectioner's sugar
- 3 tablespoons butter or margarine
- ½ teaspoon vanilla
- 1 ½–2 tablespoons milk
- Graham crackers
- Small milk carton (clean and dry)
- Candy decorations
- Sparkling sugar

1 First, make cement frosting: Combine confectioners' sugar, butter or margarine, vanilla, and milk. Mix ingredients until frosting is smooth and easy to spread. If it's too runny, just add more sugar.

2 Spread cement frosting onto 4 graham cracker squares. Press one square onto each side of the milk carton. Decorate with candy and frosting.

3 Frost 2 graham crackers and build a roof. To create the look of newly fallen snow, frost the rooftop and sprinkle with sparkling sugar.

Cozy Bookmarks

Miss Lilly would love one of these special bookmarks. Make one—or two—for your teacher, too!

Supplies:
- Felt (any color)
- Mitten and stocking templates (page 37)
- Spring curl, or salon hair clip
- Craft glue
- Glitter, stickers, fabric paint, and micro beads

1 Trace the template 4 times onto felt, and have a grown-up cut out shapes. On 2 of the cutouts, trim the top edge slightly so that these pieces are shorter than the other two.

2 Open the clip. Glue the two smaller cutouts onto the insides of the clip so the cutouts line up. Then close the clip and glue the larger cutouts onto the outsides of the clip and to the inner cutouts. Allow the glue to dry, then decorate as desired.

Gingerbread Magnet

Supplies:
- Thin, fine-grade corkboard
- Gingerbread template (page 37)
- Markers
- Craft glue
- Buttons
- Yarn and ribbon
- Magnet

Grandma and Grandpa will be excited to see this adorable magnet on the refrigerator.

1 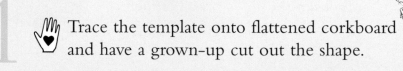 Trace the template onto flattened corkboard and have a grown-up cut out the shape.

2 Draw eyes and mouth with markers. Decorate with glue, buttons, ribbon, and yarn. Glue a magnet to the back.

Supplies:
- 1 cup cornstarch
- 2 cups baking soda
- 1½ cups water
- Paper clips
- Craft glue
- Fabric paint
- Glitter
- Rhinestones
- Ribbon

*Angelina is the star of
the ice skating show!*

1 ♥ Mix cornstarch and baking soda in a large pot. Add water. Stir until smooth. Cover and have a grown-up cook over medium heat till mixture is like mashed potatoes.

2 Turn onto a counter and cover with a damp cloth. When cool enough to handle, knead with cornstarch till smooth. Roll and cut with cookie cutters.

3 ♥ Insert an opened paper clip into the top edge of each shape. Have a grown-up bake them on a cookie sheet at 275° until hard, about 20 minutes.

4 When cool, decorate with glue and glitter, fabric paint, and rhinestones. Tie a pretty ribbon through the paper clip loop to hang these pretty ornaments on your tree.

19

Sweet Spice Ornaments

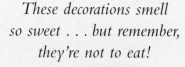

Supplies:

- One 4-ounce can ground cinnamon
- ¾ cup applesauce
- 2 tablespoons Elmer's glue
- 1 tablespoon each nutmeg, cloves (optional)
- Drinking straw

These decorations smell so sweet . . . but remember, they're not to eat!

1 Combine all ingredients except for the straw. Mix with hands for 2 to 3 minutes, until smooth. Divide dough into 4 equal portions.

2 Roll each portion out between sheets of wax paper to ¼- or ½-inch thick. Peel off top sheet of wax paper.

3 Cut with cookie cutters and use a straw to make a hole in the top center of each shape. Peel away the excess.

4 Let dry at room temperature for several days. For even drying and to prevent curling, flip the shapes once each day.

5 If desired, use fabric paint or permanent markers to decorate.

6 Use finished shapes as ornaments or gift tags. Tie ribbon through the holes to hang or attach to gifts.

Glitter and Glue Ornaments

Fast and easy . . . with sparkly results!

Supplies:
- Plastic wrap or wax paper
- Paper plate
- Craft glue
- Lots of glitter

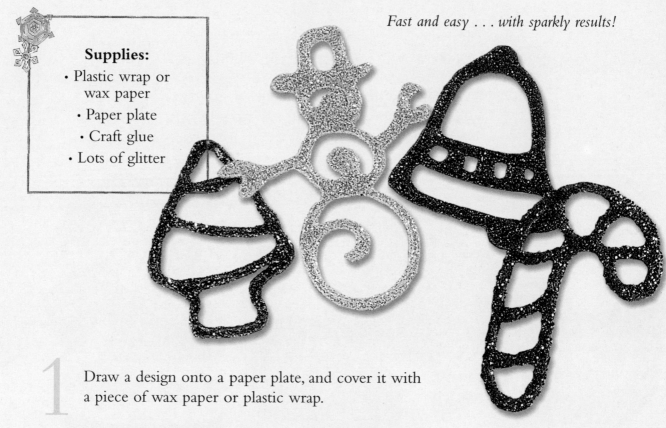

1 Draw a design onto a paper plate, and cover it with a piece of wax paper or plastic wrap.

2 Trace the image with a thick line of glue onto the wax paper or plastic wrap. Sprinkle with lots of glitter and let dry for several hours or up to a day. Peel from paper and hang.

Nifty Noodle Snowflakes

*Use your noodles to create
fanciful snowflake decorations
for your window or tree.*

Supplies:
- Pasta (rotini, wagon wheel, fettucine)
- Craft glue
- Acrylic paints
- Shimmery acrylic glaze
- String or ribbon

1 Arrange pasta into snowflake shapes. Glue shapes together with tacky craft glue and let dry on wax paper or a paper plate.

2 Paint with acrylic paints, and, if desired, accent with shimmery glaze. Let dry. Have an adult hang with string or ribbon.

23

Tiny Tree

Decorate a pint-sized version of Angelina's holiday tree.

Supplies:
- Pinecone
- Small clay pot
- Acrylic paints
- Pipe cleaner
- Craft glue
- Sequins or mini pom-poms

1 Paint pinecone and clay pot with acrylic paint. Let dry.
Have an adult help you wrap a pipe cleaner around as a garland.
Line inner rim of the pot with glue and set pinecone inside.

2 Use dots of glue to attach sequins or mini
pom-poms for ornaments. Top with a sequin star.

24

Supplies:
- Stale bread
- Drinking straw
- Yarn
- Peanut butter
- Mixed birdseed
- Currants

Hang some ornaments outside, too!
The birds will thank you.

1 Cut shapes out of slices of stale bread with cookie cutters. Use a straw to make a hanging hole in each shape. Thread yarn through each hole.

2 Spread peanut butter onto shapes, and sprinkle with birdseed. Decorate with sunflower seeds and currants. Let bread dry, then hang outside for the birds.

25

Bend 'n Bead Tree

Supplies:
- Pipe cleaner
- Beads
- Star-shaped bead or button

Angelina remembers that Christmas is a time for giving when she brings a tree and goodies to Mr. Bell.

1 String beads along a pipe cleaner. Add a star bead to one end. Bend the pipe cleaner around each end bead to hold it in place.

2 Form the beaded pipe cleaner into a tree shape.

Quiet Little Mouse

. . . not even a mouse!

1 Paint a medicine cup or nutshell. Let dry. Glue one large pom-pom inside, then a medium one for a head, and two small ones for ears.

2 Glue on micro bead features and a bent pipe cleaner tail. Finish with a felt handle on the medicine cup to make a teacup or add a pink ribbon for the nutshell. Glue into place. Let dry.

27

Angelina's Crown

Supplies:
- 8½-by-11-inch glittery craft paper
- Template (page 39)
- Craft glue
- Double-sided tape
- Pipe cleaners
- Beads and rhinestones

1 Trace the template onto glittery craft paper and have a grown-up cut it out. Make sure you have a 2-inch strip of paper left over.

2 Tape 3 bent pipe cleaners and 3 pipe cleaners with beaded ends to the back side of crown, as shown. Attach enough of the leftover 2-inch paper strip to fit the crown securely over your head.

...and Fairy Wand

On the night of her first performance, Angelina waited backstage with her crown on and her wand ready . . .

Supplies:
- 4 cups marshmallows
- ¼ cup butter
- 1 cup white chocolate chips
- 6 cups crisp rice cereal
- Star cookie cutter
- Wooden dowels
- Candies or edible glitter
- Cellophane
- Curly ribbon

1 Have a grown-up microwave first 3 ingredients on high for 3 to 3 ½ minutes or till melted, stirring after 2 minutes. Once the mixture is done microwaving, add cereal and stir.

2 Once mixture is cool enough, press it into a lightly greased pan. Use cookie cutters to make large stars until mixture is used up. Insert a dowel to make each star a wand!

3 Decorate with candies, white chocolate chips, and edible glitter. Cool for one hour. If desired, wrap in cellophane, then add curly ribbons.

29

The Nutcracker Suite

Put on your own little performance of The Nutcracker!

Supplies:

- Wooden clothespin
- Acrylic paints
- Pipe cleaners
- Wide wire-edged ribbon
- Tacky craft glue
- Small pom-poms
- Colored pearl beads
- Gold braid trim
- Clay (optional)

1 Paint clothespin white and add colorful toe shoes at the bottom. Let dry. Wrap one pipe cleaner around upper body and bend ends for arms. If your pipe cleaner is too long, curl ends to make hands. Wrap lower body with another pipe cleaner, tucking in edges.

2 Have a grown-up cut a section of ribbon that's big enough for a skirt for your mouse. On one edge, pull wires at each end to gather fabric in the middle. Wrap the ribbon around upper clothespin section and twist together in back to secure.

3 Glue on pom-poms and beads to make a face and ears, and a snip of gold braid for a crown. Let dry. If your mouse won't stand by herself, add clay feet to the bottom of your clothespin.

Mrs. Mouseling's Christmas Cookies

Ingredients:
- 1 stick chilled butter
- ¾ cup flour
- ¼ cup sugar
- 1 teaspoon vanilla
- Colored sugars

Make these cookies for your family and friends. The recipe is so simple, you will have so much fun!

1 Grease 2 cookie sheets with butter or margarine. Preheat oven to 300°.

2 Cut butter into small pieces in a bowl. Add flour and sugar. Mix together with a fork and then with your fingers, till dough is crumbly.

3 Add vanilla and mix well with a fork. Then gently squeeze the mixture into a ball.

4 Sprinkle flour onto a countertop and knead the dough into a smooth, firm ball. Roll with a floured rolling pin till dough is about ¼-inch thick.

5 Cut shapes with cookie cutters. Place shapes onto greased cookie sheets and decorate with colored sugar.

6 Have a grown-up bake cookies at 300° for 20 to 25 minutes or till they're light golden. Cool for 5 minutes on the cookie sheet before moving to a wire rack to cool.

Christmas Crackers

Christmas crackers are a special holiday tradition in Angelina's village. Make some to add fun to your Christmas or New Year's celebration.

Supplies:
- Cardboard rolls
- Crepe paper
- Clear tape
- Curling ribbon
- Small surprises

1 For each cracker, roll a 4 ½-inch cardboard tube (such as a toilet paper roll) in 2 layers of crepe paper. Leave 3 inches of paper at each end. Tape the middle.

2 Gather paper at one end and tie with ribbon. Pour confetti, small toys, or treats into the other end, and tie with ribbon. When it's time to celebrate, pop open by tugging at both ends.

Snowy Day Fun

The weather outside might be frightful, but the fun that a snowy day brings can really be delightful! You don't even have to bundle up in a snowsuit to enjoy some of these winter fun ideas.

Play in the snow—inside!

Bring in a big bowl of clean, fluffy snow. Dump it onto a cookie sheet and get out some sandbox toys, little cars, and mini people. Have a ball inside in the snow—while it lasts!

Unfold an indoor blizzard!

Fold clean coffee filters into fourths, and cut out teeny, tiny shapes along the edges to make snowflakes. Tint the flakes by dipping them in cups of colored water. String them onto thread for a pretty (easy!) garland.

Paint your snowscape a rainbow of bright colors

For some colorful outdoor fun, fill several squirt bottles with water, add a few squirts of a different food color to each, and shake well. Then go outside and decorate your snow!

Tips for Parents

Try these ways to share your values—and time—with your children this holiday season.

Create a few simple family traditions.

Traditions don't have to be elaborate. They can be something simple, like decorating cookies, making ornaments, or drinking hot cocoa—anything a child can count on doing every year.

The security of having a routine during the holidays, just like at every other time of year, is comforting to small children.

Minimize the hoopla.

Wait until early to mid-December to start involving your children in holiday preparations. Also, try to plan something special for children to look forward to *after* Christmas Day, such as going to see *The Nutcracker*, ice-skating as a family, or enjoying a special New Year's dinner. This takes the focus off the anticipation of gifts, and spreads the excitement to other activities.

Teach your child the joy of giving.

By helping your child make simple gifts for others, you are giving her some of the greatest gifts of all—the feeling of satisfaction and a valuable lesson in sharing goodwill.

Tips for Kids

Punch out templates on the following pages and put them somewhere for safekeeping until you're ready to make the crafts.

Attach the gift tags on the following pages to your creations to make special gifts for family and friends. Use a sticker to attach each gift tag, or punch a hole in the tag and tie with ribbon. Decorate your holiday crafts or packages with the extra snowflake stickers.

Aluminum foil makes a sparkly gift wrap. Take a large piece of foil and use it to wrap gifts—all by yourself! You can tuck corners into place and seal with some tape. For a beautiful finish, add some of Angelina's snowflake stickers and a pretty bow!

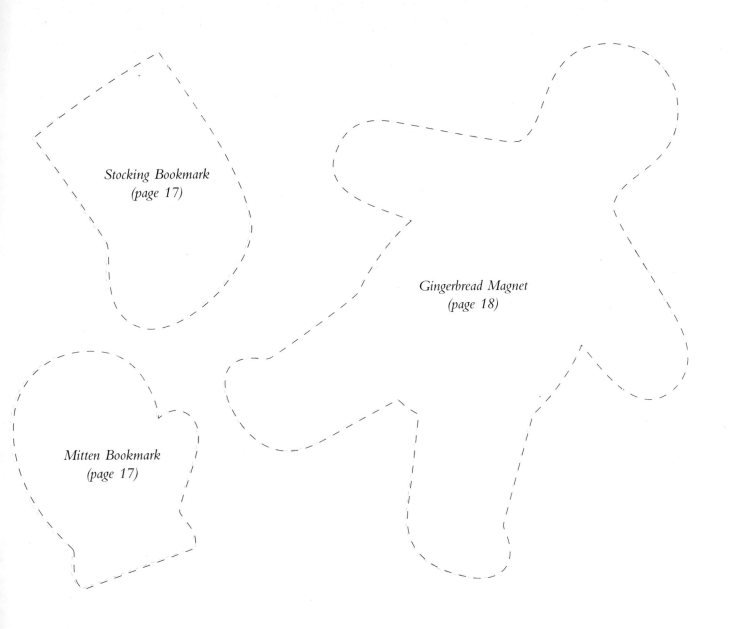

Stocking Bookmark
(page 17)

Gingerbread Magnet
(page 18)

Mitten Bookmark
(page 17)

Angelina's Crown
(page 28)

To:———————————
From:———————————

To:———————————
From:———————————

To:———————————
From:———————————

To:———————————
From:———————————

To:———————————
From:———————————

To:———————————
From:———————————

To:————————

From:————————

To:————————

From:————————

To:————————

From:————————

To:————————

From:————————

To:————————

From:————————

To:————————

From:————————